Valentine Hearts
Holiday Poetry

An I Can Read Book™

Valentine Hearts

Holiday Poetry

selected by Lee Bennett Hopkins
pictures by JoAnn Adinolfi

HarperCollins*Publishers*

ACKNOWLEDGMENTS

Thanks are due to the following for use of works that appear in this collection:

Curtis Brown, Ltd., for "Mom's Lunchbox Love" by Rebecca Kai Dotlich; copyright © 2005 by Rebecca Kai Dotlich. "For Her" and "Yes, I Did!" by Lee Bennett Hopkins; copyright © 2005 by Lee Bennett Hopkins. All reprinted by permission of Curtis Brown, Ltd.

Maria Fleming for "Red" and "Sweet Talk." Used by permission of the author, who controls all rights.

Peggy Robbins Janousky for "Love Note for Leo." Used by permission of the author, who controls all rights.

Linda Kulp for "Singing Valentine." Used by permission of the author, who controls all rights.

Ann Whitford Paul for "Valentine." Used by permission of the author, who controls all rights.

Heidi Bee Roemer for "Valentine Matchup." Used by permission of the author, who controls all rights.

Marilyn Singer for "Heart Art." Used by permission of the author, who controls all rights.

HarperCollins®, 🐿®, and I Can Read Book® are trademarks of HarperCollins Publishers Inc.

Valentine Hearts: Holiday Poetry
Text copyright © 2005 by Lee Bennett Hopkins
Illustrations copyright © 2005 by JoAnn Adinolfi

Library of Congress Cataloging-in-Publication Data
Valentine hearts : holiday poetry / selected by Lee Bennett Hopkins ; pictures by JoAnn Adinolfi.— 1st ed.
    p. cm. — (An I can read book)
  ISBN 0-06-008057-4 — ISBN 0-06-008058-2 (lib. bdg.)
  1. Valentine's Day—Juvenile poetry. 2. Children's poetry, American. [1. Valentine's Day—Poetry. 2. American poetry—Collections.] I. Hopkins, Lee Bennett. II. Adinolfi, JoAnn, ill. III. Series.
PS595.V3V35 2005
811.008'0334—dc28   2003027794

1 2 3 4 5 6 7 8 9 10
❖
First Edition

To Joan C. Stevenson—
with
all my heart
—L.B.H.

For Gemma—my little girl with the big heart
—J.A.

CONTENTS

Mom's Lunchbox Love

BY REBECCA KAI DOTLICH

O, it's Valentine's Day,

a surprise from the start—

my sandwich is cut

in the shape

of a heart.

Heart Art

BY MARILYN SINGER

The lace is all crooked,

There's ink on my dress.

Instead of a heart,

I am making a mess.

I'm littered with glitter,

I'm covered with glue.

I should sign

VALENTINE

10

And send ME off to you!

Valentine

BY ANN WHITFORD PAUL

*H*ere's my valentine.

*E*njoy the rhyme.

*A*nd then

*R*eply in heart-beat

*T*ime.

Say you'll be mine.

Golden Heart

BY ANONYMOUS

Golden heart

Be on your way.

Go, speed along

To sweetly say

That on this good

St. Valentine's Day

A heart is meant

To give away.

Valentine Matchup

BY HEIDI BEE ROEMER

Like *pea* and *pod*

or *bird* and *feather*,

certain words

go well together.

There's *hand* with *glove*,

and *sock* with *shoe*,

but best of all

is *me* with *you*.

Sweet Talk

BY MARIA FLEMING

White hearts.

Green hearts.

Yellow, purple, pink.

Telling secrets

Spelled in sugared ink:

"Be Mine."

"For Keeps."

"It's True."

"How Sweet."

Tiny love notes

Good enough to eat.

For Her

BY LEE BENNETT HOPKINS

I am sending

a card

to our

school crossing guard

to let her know

how glad I am

that she's always there

to help

hurry-hurry-hurry feet

safely

cross

a busy

street.

Singing Valentine

BY LINDA KULP

Outside my window
on the icy ground below
a little bird sings:

"Chick-a-dee

          dee

              dee

Chick-a-dee

      dee

         dee."

22

A valentine melody

just for me!

Love Note for Leo

BY PEGGY ROBBINS JANOUSKY

I'm writing a love note for Leo.

I'm using my prettiest pad.

I'm writing a love note for Leo.

The best dog a girl ever had.

I'm writing a love note for Leo.

I'm printing with squiggles and bows.

I'm using my very best writing.

I can't wait to see his face glow.

I'm writing a love note for Leo.

I'm gluing on bangles and beads.

I know that he'd love

Every word that I wrote

If only my Leo could read.

Red

BY MARIA FLEMING

It's Valentine's Day,

and everything's red:

red flowers, red candies,

red cupids with bows,

red Valentine hearts

(a million of those).

Red, red, red.

Everything's red,

except me. I'm blue.

Because I didn't get

a Valentine

from

you.

Somebody

BY ANONYMOUS

Somebody

loves you

deep and true.

If I weren't

so bashful

I'd tell you

who.

Yes, I Did!

BY LEE BENNETT HOPKINS

I didn't think I got

a card from you—

but tonight

when I found it

tucked inside my spelling book,

I shouted:

HIP-

HIP-

HOO-

RAY

'cause
this was my
very best
Valentine's Day.

Index of Authors and Titles